Moonlight Riders

LINDA CHAPMAN

ORCHARD BOOKS

First published in Great Britain in 2022 by The Watts Publishing Group

1 3 5 7 9 10 8 6 4 2

A CIP catalogue record for this book
is available from the British Library.

ISBN 978 1 40836 677 6

Printed and bound in Great Britain by Clays Ltd, Elcograf S.p.A

The paper and board used in this book are made from wood from responsible sources.

Orchard Books
An imprint of
Hachette Children's Group
Part of The Watts Publishing Group Limited
Carmelite House
50 Victoria Embankment
London EC4Y 0DZ

An Hachette UK Company
www.hachette.co.uk
www.hachettechildrens.co.uk

Moonlight Riders

Fire Horse

LINDA CHAPMAN

To Natalie Barsby, the wonderful trainer of the QHPC mounted games teams, the parents who help and of course all the very enthusiastic members of the QHPC mounted games teams, past and present.

Linda

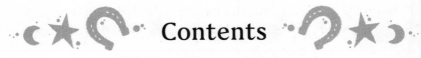 # Contents

CHAPTER ONE

Amara cantered along the narrow lane. The sun was shining and the yellow daffodils in the hedgerow were nodding their heads in the spring breeze. Amara slowed to a trot as she rounded the bend. She straightened her back, remembering what she had read about good riding, and set off once more. Amara wasn't riding a real horse, she was on her own two feet, but in her imagination she was mounted on a beautiful black pony with a white star called Midnight. She leapt over a puddle, imagining they were soaring over a jump. With her two long brown plaits bouncing on her shoulders, she cantered around a bend in the lane and then stopped.

On the left-hand side there was a riding stables. A driveway led up a slope, past a bungalow with a pretty front garden, to a metal gate. Beyond the gate, Amara could see a stable block with each of the doors painted a different colour. A sign read *Moonlight Stables,* and underneath were the words *Proprietor: Jill Reed.*

The Easter holidays had just started and Amara's parents had said it was OK for her to ask if the riding school needed any help, but now she was actually there, she could feel her tummy twisting into nervous knots.

Maybe she wouldn't go in after all. She could go for a walk instead and pat the friendly ponies over the fence, just like she had done every day since her family had moved into the cottage up the lane six weeks ago. *But I want to do more than that,* she thought longingly. *I want to help look after the ponies.*

She hugged the riding hat she was carrying to her chest. Her parents had given it to her for her ninth birthday almost two years ago and it was her most precious possession.

I can do this, she thought firmly. *The worst that can happen is they'll say no, and fingers crossed they won't!*

Just then, there was the sound of clattering hooves and two riders came around the corner – a woman and a girl.

"Get out of the way!" snapped the woman, who had black hair held back in a hairnet under her riding hat. She rode her horse straight towards Amara, who had to jump back quickly to avoid being trampled. The girl gave Amara a snooty look as she trotted past. For a moment, Amara wondered if she wanted to help at a riding school where the people were so rude. But the two riders rode on past the driveway and then Amara caught sight of a name in gold printed on the back of the girl's burgundy polo shirt: *Storm Stables.*

They're from a different stables, Amara realised in relief as the riders headed into the woods at the end of the lane.

Taking a deep breath, she walked up the driveway. There was no one around, just a wheelbarrow piled with straw. Two horses looked out over their stable doors. Amara started to walk over to them but then she heard the stamp of a hoof and glancing to the right, she saw a beautiful black pony tied to a hitching rail. Her breath caught in her throat. He was just like her imaginary pony, Midnight, apart from not having a white star. His mane and tail were thick and silky and his dark eyes were large and curious.

Amara had never seen the pony before but for some reason she felt like she recognised him and, even more strangely, he pricked his ears and whickered as if he recognised *her*. She walked over and he started to nuzzle her hands, his lips velvet-soft.

"What are you doing?" a voice rapped out.

Amara swung round. A slim woman was coming out of a wooden building with a sign

above the door that said *Tack Room* and *Office.* She had chin-length dark blonde hair and green eyes, and looked about the same age as Amara's mum.

"I . . . I'm sorry. I . . . um . . . just came to . . . well . . ." All the things she wanted to say about helping just seemed to disappear from Amara's head as she met the woman's sharp gaze.

"Hat on, please," the woman interrupted,

pointing at Amara's riding hat. "I'm Jill Reed and no one under fourteen is allowed on my yard without a riding hat. Put your hat on, get your words together and tell me why you're here."

Feeling horribly embarrassed, Amara did as she was told. "My name's Amara. I live down the lane. I came to see if you needed any help with the ponies," she gabbled. The black pony nuzzled her arm and it made her feel better.

Jill gave her an assessing look. "Can you ride? Have you had much experience?"

Amara wished she could say yes, she could ride brilliantly and she'd had loads of experience helping in a stables, but reluctantly she told the truth. "I used to ride my friend's pony. Her mum gave me some lessons, which is why I've got a riding hat, but I've never been to a riding school. My mum and dad couldn't afford that, but now Mum's got a new job she's said I can start having some lessons in the summer once we've settled in. The thing is, I don't want to wait that long." She was aware her words were starting to rush out. "Could I help here? I just want to be with ponies."

Jill studied her for a moment and then, to Amara's amazement, she gave a brief nod. "All right, I'll give you a trial this morning – provided that's OK with your parents. I run a riding club here where people help out in exchange for lessons. You might be able to join that."

Delight rushed through Amara. "That would be amazing! Thank you!"

"I haven't said you definitely can," Jill warned her. "Let's see how you get on. But first I need to speak to your parents. Let's call them."

Once Jill had phoned Amara's mum and checked she was happy for her to help for the morning, she showed Amara round and set her to work.

First, there were nets to stuff with sweet-smelling hay, then buckets to fill with water and stables to muck out. Amara carried bucket after bucket of fresh water from the trough to the stables. The buckets were heavy and she spilled quite a lot of water down her wellies, but she ignored her squelchy socks and she even felt a smile on her face when she was forking dirty straw into a wheelbarrow. She was just so happy to be with the horses and ponies!

The stable block that she had seen from the lane had three horses – Logan, Sylka and Apollo – and five cute ponies – Pippin, Pepper, Bella, Blue and Zak. There was also another block of nine stables tucked away in a quieter spot in the yard, with a track that led down to a grassy meadow that was bordered by high hedges. Jill called that block the Meadow Stables. The black pony

Amara had seen when she first arrived had a stable there. His name was Ember.

All the ponies in the Meadow Stables were beautiful, but Amara felt her eyes constantly being drawn to Ember. Halfway through the morning, she stopped to give him some fuss and let herself imagine riding him, picturing them soaring over jumps together and cantering across sunlit fields.

As she stroked him, Ember breathed gently

on her face. Knowing it was the way ponies made friends, she blew very gently back into his nostrils. He blew back and she giggled, only moving away from him when she heard a splash from the stable next door.

She went to the door and looked over it. The stable door had *Tide* written across it and inside a pretty grey pony was staring at a puddle beside her water bucket.

"Oh, Tide, you've spilled your water!" said Amara, opening the door – but then she stopped in surprise. Tide's bucket was still full to the brim. "Weird," she muttered. "Where did the water come from?"

Getting a yard brush from the rack outside, Amara swept the water out of the stable.

Rose, a stocky chestnut Welsh pony who had the stable next to Tide, came to her door and Amara saw she had pink cherry blossom caught in her creamy mane. Amara grinned "Hey, Rose. You must have rolled in blossom when you were in the meadow this morning." Leaning the broom against the stable wall, she used her fingers to comb out the pink flower heads. "There, that's much better," she said when all the blossom was out.

"Amara!" Jill called her. "Can you help me?"

"Coming!" Amara put the broom away in the equipment rack and took a last look at the ponies. She blinked. There was more pink blossom in Rose's mane. But she was sure she had removed it all. As she watched, another flower seemed to appear out of nowhere. She stared. That couldn't have just happened, could it?

"Amara!" Jill called again.

Shooting one last wondering look at Rose, Amara hurried away.

CHAPTER TWO

The rest of the morning flew by. Amara had just finished grooming Pippin when Jill came to find her. "So, Amara, have you enjoyed this morning?" she asked.

"Oh yes!" said Amara.

A smile softened Jill's usual no-nonsense expression. "Well, I'm pleased to tell you that you've passed your trial. You're a very hard worker, you listen, you clearly love ponies and you don't make mistakes twice," she said, nodding at Amara's hat approvingly. "If you'd like to come and help here in exchange for rides then that's fine by me."

"Really?" Amara gasped, excitement exploding inside her. "Oh, yes please! I'd love to help!"

Jill's smile widened. "Excellent. You'll need to join the Moonlight Stables riding club." She handed her an envelope. "Here are the forms. As soon as your parents have signed them, you can help whenever you like."

"Can I come back this afternoon?" Amara asked eagerly. "I can get my mum to sign them right away."

"That's fine by me," said Jill. "I've got some spare time because of all your help this morning, so you can have a riding lesson if you'd like."

"Can . . . can I ride Ember?" Amara asked excitedly.

Jill shook her head. "No, I don't use the ponies in the Meadow Stables for lessons. They're games ponies."

Amara didn't understand. "Games ponies?" she echoed.

"As well as having the riding school, I train a mounted games team. Do you know what mounted games are?" Jill asked.

Amara nodded. She'd watched mounted games competitions at the Horse of the Year Show on TV. Teams of four ponies and riders took part in lots of different races. They had to weave through poles; pick up flags, bottles and mugs from one place and put them down in another; negotiate obstacles; and vault on and off the ponies at a gallop.

The winning team was awarded points for each race and at the end of eight races, the team with the most points won. It was really exciting to watch.

"My team competes against other teams in a local league," said Jill. "I try and find the perfect rider for each pony in the squad and when I'm sure I've got the right match, then that pony is only ever ridden by that rider so they develop a real bond." She gave Amara a thoughtful look. "Who knows, maybe one day I'll invite you to join."

Amara was so overcome by the thought that she didn't know what to say.

Jill smiled. "I'll see you this afternoon."

Amara walked home in a daze. It had been so much better than she had hoped! Her thoughts were full of ponies, particularly

Ember. She pictured his beautiful sleek head, his dark eyes, his pricked ears. Had Jill found his perfect rider yet?

Maybe it could be me, she thought excitedly.

She dreamed about it all the way home, and almost walked past her house. Pear Tree Cottage, where she had recently moved with her parents, was at the end of a row of small brick cottages, standing close to where the lane joined the main road. Turning right at the top of the lane took you to the High Street and the shops and schools of Eastwall. Turning left led to the countryside.

Amara went round to the back door. Her mum – who had recently started a new job as Head of English at the local secondary school – was marking books at the kitchen

table while her dad was making a pile of cheese and pickle sandwiches.

"Here she is," Amara's dad said as Amara opened the door. "We were wondering when you'd be home."

"Did you have fun?" her mum asked, looking up.

"It was amazing!" Amara's blue eyes shone as she told her parents all about her morning at the stables.

"Jill – that's the owner – said she's going to give me a lesson this afternoon," she finished. "You just need to sign the papers so I can join her riding club, and she also said that maybe one day I can join her mounted games squad!"

Amara's dad laughed as he carried over the sandwiches. "I'm guessing from your smile that's a good thing?"

Amara beamed. "It is." Looking at the plate of cheese and pickle sandwiches, she suddenly realised how hungry she was. She washed her hands and wolfed down her lunch. Afterwards, she helped her dad clear away while she told him and her mum more about the ponies.

"Did you meet any people there or was it

just ponies?" her mum asked.

"Just ponies – and Jill," said Amara. "Jill said Monday is the quietest day because the riding school horses and ponies have a rest day after the weekend."

Her dad tweaked the end of one of her plaits. "I'm just glad it worked out for you, Ams. I'm proud of you for going there on your own to ask if you could help."

"I was a bit nervous before I went in," Amara admitted. "But I'm so glad I did it. I'm going to be the best helper Moonlight Stables has ever had!"

When Amara got back to the stables, Jill was riding Apollo, her retired racehorse, in the riding arena. "Hi, Amara," she called. "Can you check the buckets and then fetch Bella's tack? You'll be riding her for your lesson."

Amara set to work, her heart lifting as Ember whinnied to her. She fed him a carrot she'd brought from home. He nudged her with his nose, as if asking for more. Amara grinned. "That's all for now, beautiful. You can have another later." She topped up his water bucket then checked the other stables.

Tide's bucket was full. The grey pony came over and nuzzled her hands. To Amara's surprise, the pony's lips were damp, as if she had just been drinking. Amara took another look at the water bucket, but it was full up to the brim. Strange. Maybe Jill had already topped it up?

She made her way along the other Meadow Stables, checking the water buckets in Rose,

Cloud and Forest's stables. When she went into Sandy's stable, she found a pile of sand by the door. Amara frowned. She was sure it hadn't been there this morning.

Amara topped up Sandy's water and went to Sirocco's stable next door but just as she undid the bolt, a gust of wind rushed past her and the door flew wide open, knocking the water bucket out of her hand and

banging into the stable wall.

Amara looked round in astonishment. The wind had just blown out of nowhere and now it was gone. A prickle ran down her spine as she turned slowly back to the stables. Was there something strange about these ponies?

Don't be silly, she told herself quickly. *They're just normal ponies. After all, what else could they be?*

CHAPTER THREE

Amara was excited for her riding lesson. Bella, the pony she was riding, was small and shaggy with a coat the colour of a conker.

"Right, let's get started before the games squad arrive," said Jill once she had adjusted Amara's stirrups to the right length. "They train every afternoon in the holidays." She checked that the girth was tight so that the saddle wouldn't slip. "OK. Off you go."

It was wonderful to be riding again! Amara

couldn't stop smiling as she rode Bella around the arena, or the school as Jill called it. She tried to remember everything she knew – sit up, look ahead, heels down.

"Good," said Jill after Amara had been trotting round for ten minutes. "You might not have had lessons at a riding school, but you've got naturally good balance and light hands."

Amara glowed at the praise.

"I think we should test that balance a bit more," said Jill, and to Amara's surprise she took the stirrups off the saddle. Then she went to the other side of the school and started to lay four wooden poles out in a line.

"Who are you?" a voice demanded.

Amara looked round and saw a tall, pretty girl, about a year older than her, coming over to the fence. She had long, curly blonde hair tied back in a ponytail and pale green eyes. She was smartly dressed in dark grey riding tights and a green top printed with the name of an expensive riding brand. Her green hat silk matched her top.

Amara smiled. "Hi, I'm Amara."

"Amara?" The girl echoed, pulling a face. "What kind of name's that?" Amara blinked at her unfriendly tone. "Oh no, you're not a new member of the riding club, are you?" the girl said, rolling her eyes as if it was a really lame thing to be.

"I am. Are you a member too?" Amara asked.

"Me?" The girl gestured at her riding clothes. "Do I look like I need to work for lessons? No, my family can actually afford to pay for my lessons."

Amara felt a spark of anger. There was no need for the girl to be so horrible. "Well, lucky you," she retorted. "It doesn't make you better than me though!"

Just then Jill walked over. "Hi, Zara. Are you getting to know Amara?"

Zara suddenly put on a super-sweet smile. "Yes, she was just telling me she's joined the riding club. That's so nice." Amara gaped, unable to believe how two-faced she was being.

Amara was very aware of Zara watching her for the rest of the lesson. It made her feel tense. It didn't help that riding without stirrups was hard. Walking was fine but trotting was very bouncy.

After a while, Zara was joined by a shorter

girl with auburn hair and brown eyes. She was also pretty and smartly dressed, and Amara saw her giggling with Zara as she had to grab the front of the saddle to stop herself bouncing off Bella's back. She was very relieved when Jill let her have her stirrups back.

"You did really well for your first time without stirrups," Jill said. "Now, let's finish with a jump."

Amara hadn't done much jumping but she loved it. Forgetting all about the annoying girls at the side, Amara soon lost herself in the feeling of cantering round and flying over the jump.

"Excellent!" said Jill as Amara brought the pony to a halt, patting her affectionately on the neck. "That was a great first lesson. Can you take Bella in and sponge her down?"

Amara nodded and Jill waved to the side of the school. "OK, you lot, come and help me set up!"

Glancing round, Amara saw that Zara and her friend had been joined by a boy and a girl. She gave a start as she recognised them – they were both in her class at school! The boy was called Alex Brahler and the girl was Imogen Fairfax. She didn't know them very well yet. It had been hard joining a new school in the middle of Year 6. Everyone already had their friendship groups and although most of the girls and boys in her class, including Alex and Imogen, had been friendly, only Kalini, who she sat beside, had become a real friend. Kalini loved ponies as much as Amara did! She was away on holiday with her family for two weeks but Kalini was already planning on joining the riding club when she got home.

Imogen and Alex walked over with Zara and her friend. Amara tensed. Would they be horrible like Zara? But to her relief, they both smiled.

"Hi, Amara," Imogen said, pushing her glasses up her nose. "I didn't know you liked ponies."

"I love them,' said Amara, patting Bella.

"You did that jump really well," said Alex.

"Thanks," said Amara, pleased.

"For a beginner, maybe," Zara said snidely. "But you should have seen her bouncing around without stirrups. It was like watching a sack of potatoes wobbling round, wasn't it, Daniela?"

Daniela nodded. "Totally. Poor Bella."
They walked on, sniggering.

Imogen sighed. "Just ignore them," she told Amara. "They're cousins and as mean as each other . . . "

"They're good riders though," said Alex, interrupting her. "Particularly Zara – they're just really annoying."

"Imogen! Alex! Less chatting, more action, please!" Jill shouted.

"We'd better go," said Alex, grinning at Amara and dragging Imogen off to help.

By the time Amara had finished washing Bella off, the mounted games equipment was set up in the school but the rideres had all disappeared. Hearing voices coming from the Meadow Stables, she headed that way. Alex, Imogen, Daniela and Zara had been joined by a small ginger-haired girl who looked about nine, and two teenagers, one girl and one boy. They had tied the ponies to the hitching rail. Amara's heart plummeted when she saw that Zara was grooming Ember.

"Hey!" Imogen called. "Everyone, this is Amara. She goes to school with me and Alex and she's just joined the riding club. Amara, this is Bea." She pointed to the younger girl who was grooming the palomino pony, Sandy. "And that's Ollie over there, grooming Sirocco." The teenage boy with spiky dark red hair flashed her a grin. "And Jasmine with Cloud."

The teenage girl, who had thick brown hair tied back in a plait, smiled. "Hi, Amara. Nice to meet you!"

Amara smiled back. "Are you all part of the mounted games squad?"

Zara rolled her eyes. "No, we're just grooming the mounted games ponies for fun," she said sarcastically.

Amara blushed.

"Yeah, we're all part of the squad," said Ollie, shooting an exasperated look at Zara.

"Are you interested in joining? It would be good to have someone new. Jas and I are almost too old for the team."

"You have to stop doing team events in our local league when you're fourteen," Jasmine explained. "Forest is old enough now to start training." She nodded to the dark brown pony who was still in his stable. "Maybe you could ride him."

Amara sneaked a look over at Ember. She really, really wanted to ride him but if Zara had already been picked as his rider then she guessed that was never going to happen. She went over and stroked Forest's soft nose. "I'd love that."

"After seeing you ride today, I don't think Forest would!" said Zara. She shot a look at Daniela, who spluttered with laughter.

"Don't be so mean," said Imogen, frowning at them.

Amara turned her back on Zara and Daniela, refusing to let them get to her.

"So, how does it work?" she asked Imogen. "I mean, how does Jill pick a pony's perfect rider?"

"Um . . . well . . . she . . ." Imogen glanced at Alex.

"She just kind of does," he said quickly.

"The ponies help pick," Bea piped up.

Amara saw a flurry of quick looks being exchanged between the older riders and Bea turned bright red, her hands flying to her mouth.

"The ponies pick?" Amara echoed.

Jasmine gave a quick, high laugh. "Oh, it's just one of those silly things that Jill says. It's not true of course."

"No, no, of course not," said Ollie.

"As if the ponies would pick!" said Imogen.

"Yeah, as if!" said Alex.

Amara felt like there was some big secret that they weren't sharing with her. "Have all the ponies got their perfect riders?" she asked curiously.

"Not all of them," said Alex, moving around Rose. "Jasmine is Cloud's rider and Ollie is Sirocco's."

"I'm Tide's and Alex is Rose's," Imogen put in. "But Jill hasn't decided who will ride Sandy, Sparks, Forest or Ember yet."

"Er, excuse me. Everyone knows I am going to be Ember's rider!" snapped Zara. "No one else ever rides him but me." Her eyes were like daggers as she looked at Amara, as if warning her off. "He's mine!"

There was a moment's awkward silence.

"I think we should get these ponies tacked up, guys," Jasmine said quickly, breaking the tension. "We don't want to be late for training."

Amara helped fetch the tack and then Imogen showed Amara how to fasten protective wraps on the ponies' legs. To Amara's surprise all the riders rode in trainers.

"It's because we have to do so much running," Imogen explained. "They're special trainers with a heel. Normal trainers might get jammed in the stirrups."

Alex grabbed the front of Rose's saddle and threw himself on to her back, without using the stirrups. "Time to go!"

They all vaulted on – apart from little Bea, who still needed to use a stirrup – and then they clattered away towards the school.

As Amara followed them, a fierce longing filled her. She wanted to be one of them so much. *Oh, Ember,* she thought, *I wish I was riding you.*

Almost as though he had heard her, the jet-black pony swung his head round. When Zara realised he was looking at Amara, she pulled his head round roughly and gave him a sharp kick.

Ember gave an angry snort and bucked. Zara wasn't expecting the sudden movement and she shrieked as she was thrown forward on to his neck. Ember lifted his head just before she fell off and she wriggled back down into the saddle, her cheeks burning red as everyone looked round.

"What just happened?" Imogen asked.

"Nothing. It was just Ember being stupid," snapped Zara. She glared furiously at Amara, as if blaming her, and then rode away to the school.

Amara swallowed. She didn't know how it had happened but she seemed to have made an enemy of Zara.

Over the next few days, Amara spent every moment she could at the stables. The mornings were busy helping with the riding school ponies, and then in the afternoons Jill would give her a lesson and she would help with the mounted games training.

Imogen and Alex were in the riding club

too. They were friendly to Amara but she noticed they stopped talking as soon as she approached them, almost as though they didn't want her to hear what they were saying. It made her feel a bit uncomfortable. After they'd done it a few times, she decided to spend her spare time with Ember instead. She loved all the ponies but there was just something special about Ember.

On her fourth day of helping, Amara was about to head home when she heard Ember whinnying in the meadow. She stopped. It was crazy but she felt like he was calling to her. She hesitated but then, hearing him whinny again, she made up her mind. She'd give him one last hug before going home.

She hurried to the meadow. The sun was just setting and the shadows of night were starting to creep across the sky.

Ember was standing in the middle of the meadow as if he was waiting for her. Seeing her, he whickered and shook back his mane. Amara gasped as bright sparks flew out, glittering like fireflies. What was going on? Ember stamped a front hoof down hard and, to Amara's astonishment, flames shot upwards into the sky. Ember reared up on his back legs and then the most amazing thing happened – he transformed into a stunning black horse! His eyes glowed amber and – most incredible of all – his mane and tail burst into flickering orange and gold flames!

CHAPTER FOUR

Amara's heart raced in her chest. What was happening? For a moment she stood there gaping at Ember as his outline blazed against the evening sky. Then, overwhelmed by a sudden wave of panic, she turned and ran as fast as she could to Jill's bungalow.

By the time she reached it, her breath was coming in ragged gasps. She was just about to bang on the door when it opened.

"Hi, Amara," said Jill in surprise. "I was just

about to lock up. I didn't realise you were still here." She saw Amara's panicked expression. "Is everything OK?"

"No!" panted Amara. "It's Ember! He's .. . he's . . ." She struggled to find the words to explain.

"He's what?" said Jill in alarm.

"He just kind of burst into flames!" Amara blurted out. "Well, his mane and tail did, and he changed from a pony into a horse!" As the words left her, she realised how crazy she sounded.

To her astonishment, Jill smiled. "Oh. I see. I had a feeling this might happen."

Amara stared. What did she mean?

Jill reached for her coat, which was hanging on a hook beside the door. "Let's walk to the meadow. We need to talk."

Feeling like she was in some weird dream, Amara fell into step beside Jill. "What's going on?" she asked, her eyes wide.

"Before I explain, I need you to understand that what I'm about to tell you is a secret that only a small number of people know," said Jill, giving her a serious look. "Promise me that you won't tell anyone."

Amara nodded. "I promise. What . . . what happened to Ember?"

"Ember is an elemental horse," said Jill. "All the ponies in the Meadow Stable block are. It means they're magic horses," she went on at Amara's bewildered look. "Most of the time they look just like regular ponies, but they can change into a magical form. Some of them have the power of earth, others of wind, air or fire. Elemental horses use their magic to do good but, in order to do that, they need to find a special human to be their True Rider, someone they can bond with, who can help them learn how to control their magic." She glanced at Amara. "On the first day you were here, I told you that I pick the perfect rider for each pony in that stable block, but that's not strictly true. I spot people who I think might be a potential True Rider and I let them join the mounted games team to get to know the elemental ponies better – but it's the ponies themselves who choose the rider they want. When they've made their choice, they reveal their magical form to them. That's what Ember did just now. He wants you to be his True Rider."

Amara's eyes widened to the size of dinner plates. "He chose *me*?"

Jill nodded. "I can't say I'm surprised. The connection between you has been obvious from the start. But this is going to make things difficult with Zara – she thinks she is going to be Ember's True Rider."

Amara rubbed her face, trying to take it all in. "Zara knows about the elemental horses?"

"All the riders in the squad do," said Jill. "Either because they've been picked by one of the horses to be their True Rider or because they are a Legacy Rider – someone who has a parent or grandparent who was a True Rider. Zara, Daniela and Bea are all Legacy Riders. None of them have been chosen yet."

The mysterious happenings in the Meadow Stable block suddenly began to make sense. The water on Tide's floor, the sand piles only ever in Sandy's stable . . .

"Why didn't you tell me this sooner?" Amara asked.

"We have to keep the elemental horses' secret safe," said Jill. "You must too." She gave Amara a swift sideways look, a shadow crossing her eyes. "Elemental horses have so much power. If the wrong people find out, it can have tragic consequences."

"I won't tell anyone," said Amara, excitement unfurling inside her. A whole new world was suddenly opening up before her – a world of magic and ponies! "So is Ember's power fire?"

Jill smiled. "Why don't you ask him yourself?"

They rounded a bend in the path. Ember was standing near the gate, his outline

glowing golden against the dark sky. Seeing
Amara, he whinnied loudly. Breaking into
a run, she climbed over the gate, reached to
stroke him but then quickly pulled her hand
back as she realised she was about to touch
his flaming mane.

*It's all right. The flames are magic, they
can't hurt you.*

Amara's head snapped to look at Jill. But
even as she did so, she knew that it hadn't
been Jill who had spoken. She looked back at
Ember. "Was that you?" she breathed. "Did
you just speak to me?"

He nodded.

"When an elemental horse is in their
magical form, they can speak to their True
Rider using their thoughts," said Jill. "As
your bond develops you'll find Ember can

also speak to you when he's in his pony form, but that takes more practise. At first you'll just hear him occasionally."

A thrill ran through Amara. *Can you really hear me, Ember?*

His eyes met hers. In his magical form they glowed with a golden fire. *Yes.*

You're really magic? You're an elemental horse?

I am. And I've chosen you to be my True Rider, Amara. Ember reached out with his muzzle. *Will you be?*

Yes! Oh yes! Amara put her arms round his neck. The flames tickled her skin but didn't burn her.

He nuzzled her shoulder and she felt fierce happiness rushing through her. This was the most amazing thing that had ever happened!

Jill leaned against the gate. "So will you keep the elemental horses' secret safe, and help Ember use his power for good?"

"I promise I will," said Amara. "But what can you do with your power, Ember?"

Ember cantered away from her and stamped a front hoof down hard on the ground. A column of flames shot high up into the sky.

"Oh, wow," breathed Amara, hearing the crackle of the flames and feeling the burning heat from where she was standing. These weren't magical flames, they were real.

Ember stamped his feet again and the fire sank back down and disappeared.

"Fire Horses like Ember who are able to conjure large fires are very rare," said Jill. "Most Fire Horses can simply conjure sparks or a few flames. As your bond strengthens, Ember's power will increase even more. To improve your bond, I'd like you to join the squad. Training with him will help you learn how to work together."

"So I'll ride him instead of Zara?" said Amara, wondering how Zara would react to that.

Jill nodded. "Yes. From now on you will be Ember's only rider."

I never felt the bond with Zara that I feel with you, Ember told Amara. *From the moment I saw you, I knew you were the person I wanted as my True Rider. You were special.*

I felt like that about you too, Amara told him in awe.

"This is the start of an amazing journey for

you, Amara," Jill said. "But now, you should say goodnight to Ember and go home. I'll see you in the morning for riding school duties and in the afternoon for squad training." She began walking away then stopped and looked round. "I'm very glad Ember chose you," she said softly before she walked away.

Amara and Ember were left alone together, lit by the stars and the moon.

Ember bowed his head and Amara rested her forehead against his, feeling the

powerful connection that flowed between them, deep in her heart.

After a few moments, Ember wheeled away and cantered to the centre of the field. Rearing up, he shook his mane. Amara gazed at him, for the first time fully taking in his beautiful elemental form. He was still recognisably Ember, but he was taller and more majestic, his body more muscular and powerful, his mane and tail alight with flames.

I'll see you tomorrow, Amara, my True Rider!

Tomorrow, Amara promised. Her mind was still spinning with everything that had happened, but she knew for certain that she and Ember belonged to each other now.

For ever, she thought.

CHAPTER FIVE

"Is this a joke?" Zara said, putting her hands on her hips and glaring at Jill the next day. "What do you mean I'm not riding Ember?"

"Amara's going to ride him," said Jill.

"Amara? Why would you put her on Ember?" Zara gave Amara a look of deep dislike.

"It's not my decision to make," said Jill firmly.

"What?" Realisation slowly dawned on

Zara face. "You mean Ember's chosen her? He's . . ."

"Why don't you ride Forest, Zara?" Jill interrupted. "He's ready to start training now."

"But he's only four and I won't be able to gallop him like I gallop Ember!" Zara's expression hardened. "No way. That's it. You can forget me being on the squad. Come on, Daniela," she said haughtily. "This lot can stuff their stupid team!"

Daniela looked startled, but Zara gave her a fierce look and she nodded in agreement before hurrying after her cousin.

Jill heaved a sigh. "Oh dear. I hoped Zara might take it better than that."

"I feel really bad," said Amara.

Jill squeezed her shoulder. "Don't. Ember

chose you. Zara could have stayed and ridden Forest if she wanted to. It was her choice to go."

When Imogen, Alex, Ollie, Bea and Jasmine arrived, Jill pulled them to one side to explain what had happened.

"So, you're Ember's new rider," said Jasmine when they finally walked over.

"Um . . . yes," said Amara.

"Cool," said Ollie. "I mean, Zara's a pretty hard act to follow – she was one of our best riders – but I bet you'll be great too."

Nerves spiralled inside Amara. What if she let the team down? "I'll practise lots," she promised.

Jasmine, Ollie and Bea went to get their ponies out and Amara found herself with Imogen and Alex. "OMG! I can't believe you're Ember's True Rider!" Imogen squealed. "I'm so glad! Zara's an amazing rider but you're much nicer. It'll be great to have you on the team."

Amara forced a smile. She knew Imogen had meant the words kindly but hearing again how brilliant Zara was wasn't doing anything to help calm her anxiety.

"You'll be able to practise magic with us too," Imogen went on eagerly.

"It'll be awesome!" said Alex, grinning at Amara.

Amara forgot her nerves for a moment and grinned back. It really would be!

Mounted games was a lot harder than it looked. Jill had found an old pair of riding trainers for Amara and it was amazing to finally be riding Ember. However, she soon discovered he was incredibly sensitive; she only had to lean slightly one way and he would swerve in that direction. At one point when they were practising bending in and out of a line of upright poles, he turned so quickly around the final pole she almost fell off.

"Sorry," she said as he stopped so she could get straight in the saddle again.

He snorted softly and she had a feeling he was saying it didn't matter, but she felt bad that she was so much worse than anyone else on the team. The others could hang off the side of the saddle at a gallop and then right themselves with no effort at all. Jasmine and Ollie could even reach down so far they

could scoop things off the ground.

I will get better. I will practise, Amara thought with a fierce rush of determination. *I'm not going to let Ember – or the team – down.*

"OK, time to cool these ponies off," said Jill at last. "Jasmine, Ollie, Bea – you take your ponies for a walk through the woods. Imogen, Alex and Amara, why don't you untack and take your ponies down to the meadow? You could show Amara what Rose and Tide can do."

"Sure," Imogen said quickly. "Come on, Amara."

Alex grinned at her. "It's magic time!" he said.

They untacked the ponies and then Alex vaulted back on to Rose. "Let's ride down the track to the meadow," he said, using the headcollar's leadrope as a single rein.

"You mean ride them without a saddle and bridle?" said Amara.

Alex grinned. "You're not scared, are you?"

"No," Amara said quickly, not wanting to admit she did find the idea quite scary.

"We'll only walk," said Imogen. "Ember will look after you."

Amara climbed on to Ember's warm back

from the fence. It felt very strange when he walked off. Feeling unsteady, she leaned forward, holding tightly to his mane.

"Just sit back and relax," Imogen said, riding alongside her. "Let your body move with his."

Amara did as Imogen said and found it was easier.

"You'll have to learn how to gallop without a saddle and bridle so that you can take part in the Moonlight Ritual," Imogen went on as they rode down the track.

"What's the Moonlight Ritual?" asked Amara.

"Four times a year, on the night of the first full moon at the start of each new season, all True Riders take their horses out for a bareback ride in the moonlight. You shouldn't need tack if you and your horse trust each other. The ritual renews the horses' magic and strengthens their bond with their riders and—"

"It's just awesome," interrupted Alex. "Jill lets us camp in her front garden and we all ride up through the woods and gallop along the ridgeway at the top of the hill. As the full moon falls on the ponies, you can feel the power surging through them."

Imogen grinned. "Afterwards we come back and toast marshmallows round a campfire."

"And tell ghost stories," added Alex. He pulled a spooky face. "Whooooooo! Scaaaaary!"

Imogen shook her head at him. "It's really fun," she told Amara. "The next Moonlight

Ritual is a week on Saturday, just before we go back to school."

Amara made up her mind then and there that she would practise riding Ember without a saddle and bridle every single moment she could! There was no way she wanted to miss out. "So is it just the True Riders who go?"

"Yes," said Imogen. "And Jill of course. She rides Apollo. He isn't an elemental horse but he's really fast."

Amara frowned. "Why doesn't Jill have an elemental horse?"

"She had a Fire Horse called Shula when she was younger," Imogen explained. "But Shula was in an accident when Jill was seventeen. Jill doesn't like to talk about her, but after the accident she decided that she would spend her life helping other elemental horses find their True Riders."

When they got to the meadow, they rode towards a massive old oak tree that stood near the little stream that ran along one of the hedges. Its wide trunk and thick branches blocked them from the sight of anyone who might pass the gate that led on to the lane.

"Rose and I will go first!" said Alex. "She's an Earth Horse and can grow things." He rode the stocky chestnut pony away from them and then halted her, stroking her neck and concentrating hard for a few moments. It was strange to see Alex staying so still; he was usually moving and talking. He always got into trouble for that at school.

Suddenly, he clapped his heels to Rose's

sides. She leapt forwards at a canter and raced around the trunk of the tree. As she did so, bright blue buds sprang up from under her hooves. By the time she skidded to a halt there was a circle of beautiful bluebells surrounding the tree. Amara was thrilled. "Oh, wow! It's like . . . like . . ."

"Magic, I know!" grinned Imogen.

Alex raced back to them.

"That's amazing! Can she grow anything she wants?" asked Amara.

"She can, though she finds it easier to grow flowers that are natural to wherever she is," said Alex, ruffling Rose's mane. "If she tried to grow something like a desert cactus here in the meadow, the magic would take a lot more energy."

"Jill says it's because elemental horses

use the current of magic that comes from nature," explained Imogen. "So it's easier for them to do things that are natural. Tide's a Water Horse. She can make it rain even if there are no rain clouds, but because that's unnatural she finds it very tiring. It's much easier for her to control water that's already there." She dismounted and removed Tide's headcollar. "Should we show Amara what you can do, Tidey?"

Tide nodded and stared at the stream, tapping one of her front hooves on the ground. The water in the stream rushed to one spot and rose up in a sparkling column. At the top of it, the water droplets sprayed out and pattered back down into the stream like a fountain. Tide tapped her hoof harder and the column started to spin and twist,

forming a waterspout. It moved across the
surface of the stream until Tide stamped
both front hooves and then it exploded, the
water falling back down.

"That's so cool!" Amara exclaimed.

"Thanks," said Imogen, beaming. "Tide
and I have been practising really hard so she
can control her magic when she's in her pony

form. It's much easier when the horses are in their elemental form." She hugged her pony. "You're the best!" she told her.

Ember jostled Amara impatiently. "Can Ember and I have a go now?" she said eagerly.

"Sure," said Imogen. "First, you need to learn how to speak to him even when he's in his pony form."

"It's not easy," Alex warned. "You have to sit still and try not to think about anything else. It took me ages to learn how to do that."

"Touching him will help," said Imogen.

Amara placed her hand on Ember's shoulder and leaned down to look into one of his eyes. He stared back and as she focused on him, she felt the rest of the world fade away. She felt a click in her mind, as if a door had suddenly opened.

Amara?

Ember! I can hear you! Joy rushed through her as his thoughts flooded her own.

What magic should we do? he asked.

Amara remembered how Rose had formed a circle of flowers. *Let's make a circle of fire, but just really small fires,* she added, remembering the massive column of fire he had made the day before. *Do you think you can do that?*

I'm sure I can, said Ember. *But I think it will help me control the magic if you stroke my neck. Shall we try?*

Amara nodded.

There was a moment's pause and then Amara felt a feather-light tingle sweep across her skin. The tingle grew stronger until it became a sharp prickle. *It's magic,* she realised in delight, *magic flowing from Ember to me!*

Ember tapped a hoof on the ground and a small fire lit up in the grass, a few golden flames flickering. He moved his gaze slightly to the right and tapped his foot again. Another little fire appeared, and then another and another . . . until they were surrounded by a complete circle of fire. Amara felt a sudden intoxicating sense of power.

"That's awesome!" she heard Alex exclaim.

"Be careful!" warned Imogen. "Encourage Ember to keep his focus."

I will, Ember told Amara.

Amara smiled at him. *It is amazing, but maybe we'd better put the fires out now?*

He nodded and stamped both his front hooves down. Amara's heart leapt in fear as for one moment the flames suddenly surged upwards. Ember quickly stamped his hooves again and then the fires faded to nothing, leaving just a charred circle on the ground.

Amara released a trembling breath. For one horrible second she'd thought Ember had been losing control of the fire. As they turned back to the others, she felt the connection between her and Ember shut off, like a door closing.

"That was amazing," said Imogen.

Amara glowed with pride.

We did it, she thought. *We did magic! And we did it well.*

There was the sound of clattering hooves. All three ponies lifted their heads, pricking their ears as they saw Ollie, Jasmine and Bea trotting along the lane past the gate.

"Weird," said Imogen, frowning at Alex. "They're supposed to be walking to cool the ponies off, not trotting."

"Maybe something's happened. Let's go and see," said Alex. "We can leave our ponies here."

Giving their ponies a last hug, they ran back to the yard.

When they got there, they found Ollie, Jasmine and Bea talking to Jill and gesturing excitedly. Jill was frowning and looked worried.

"What's going on?" Alex demanded.

"We were out in the woods and guess who was there?" Jasmine said. She didn't wait for an answer. "Ivy Thornton!"

"She was riding that bay horse of hers
– Bolt – you know the one who bites and
kicks," said Ollie. "And she was spying on our
stable."

"We don't know that for sure," said
Jasmine.

"She was taking pictures and videos with
her phone," said Ollie. "It looked like spying
to me."

Amara felt completely confused. "Who's
Ivy Thornton?"

"The owner of Storm Stables," said Jill.

Amara remembered the rude, smartly
dressed woman she had seen the first day
she had come to Moonlight Stables. "Why
does it matter if she was in the woods taking
pictures?" she asked curiously.

Jill sighed heavily. "Because she knows

about elemental horses."

"She's a True Rider," Bea piped up.

"Not a True Rider, Bea," Jasmine corrected her. "She's a Night Rider, isn't she, Jill?"

Jill nodded. "Night Riders are True Riders who have turned bad," she explained to Amara. "They get so intoxicated by their horse's power that they start to want more power, and when they have it they use it for their own selfish gain. Ivy and I have known each other since we were at school." For a moment, Jill's face darkened and pain flashed through her eyes. "There's a lot of history between us."

"Which is why Jill has always told us that if we see her acting suspiciously we should tell her," said Ollie.

"This is the first time we've ever seen

her doing something weird though," said Jasmine.

"Why now?" Jill said, more to herself than to anyone else. "Unless . . ." Her gaze fell on Amara and her frown deepened. "Look, I need you all to be extra vigilant," she said briskly. "It may be nothing more than Ivy trying to see what we're doing here but I really don't trust her."

CHAPTER SIX

That night, Amara's dreams were full of mysterious Night Riders chasing her and Ember across fields and through woods. She was glad to wake up and get dressed.

When she got to the stables, Jill told her that there was going to be no training session that day. "I don't like to train the ponies every day; they start to get bored and don't try as hard." She smiled. "The riders too! I'm going to give Bea a jumping lesson. Ollie and

Jasmine are going to give Sirocco and Cloud a day off. I thought you, Alex and Imogen could go out for a ride in the woods."

Amara loved the idea of going out, and Imogen and Alex seemed just as happy about the plan.

"Training's fun but I love hacking too," said Imogen as they rode out of the stables after lunch and headed into the woods at the end of the lane. A bridlepath twisted through the trees. Birds sang in the branches and squirrels scampered up the trunks. Imogen and Amara rode side by side while Alex rode ahead on Rose.

"I'm bored of walking. Who wants a canter?" he called as the track widened.

"Me!" both girls replied.

The ponies set off, their hooves thudding

into the soft surface of the bridlepath. Amara leaned forwards like a jockey. It was amazing to feel the wind rushing past her.

After the canter, they turned on to a track that led upwards through the trees and came out in a field halfway up the hill. Looking down, Amara could see back to Moonlight Stables, the buildings nestled together and the ponies in the paddocks. "It's so lovely up here," she said.

Ember snorted in agreement.

"Should we have another canter?" said Alex eagerly.

"Wait!" Imogen said suddenly. "There are some other riders. Look."

Four riders had just ridden on to the hill from another bridlepath higher up – led by a small, slim woman on a bay horse. There were also three girls on stunning ponies, one with dark brown hair on an iron grey pony and . . .

"It's Zara and Daniela!" Imogen burst out. "On ponies from Storm Stables."

Zara was riding a beautiful fiery-red chestnut pony who looked like a miniature racehorse and Daniela was on a stockier, glossy bright bay pony with the thickest mane and tail Amara had ever seen.

"I can't believe they've joined Storm Stables," said Alex.

"I can," said Imogen darkly.

Amara frowned as she saw light glint off something that Ivy Thornton was holding up to her eyes. "Are those binoculars?"

"They are! She's spying on Moonlight Stables, just like Ollie and the others said she was yesterday!" said Alex.

Zara spotted them and called to Ivy. Amara saw her pointing in their direction. A feeling of foreboding swept through her as Ivy turned her binoculars on her and Ember.

"What's she doing?" she said uneasily. "Why's she looking at us?"

"I'm going to find out," said Alex impulsively.

"No, Alex!" Imogen exclaimed. "You can't just ride up to them."

"I can! Watch me!" said Alex. Clapping his heels to Rose's sides, he cantered up the hill.

"Alex!" Imogen yelled. "Come back!" But Alex ignored her.

Ivy said something to the three girls. They nodded and immediately galloped down the hill straight towards Alex, the three of them

side by side, Ivy watching from above.

"What are they doing?" said Imogen in alarm. "They're going to crash into Alex!"

"I think that's the idea!" gasped Amara.

Rose realised the danger and swerved just in time but her movement was so swift and sudden that Alex was flung from her back. He catapulted through the air and thudded into the ground.

"Alex!" Imogen shrieked, and set off at a

flat-out gallop towards him.

The three girls swept on down the hill, high-fiving each other and hooting with laughter.

To Amara's relief, Alex sat up just as Imogen reached him. He didn't look hurt. But then she had other things to think about. Ivy Thornton had urged her horse on and was galloping down the hill. She stopped right beside Ember,

"So this is the Fire Horse," Ivy said, her pale blue eyes glittering. "And you're his True Rider." Her gaze swept over Amara and she tapped her riding crop against one of her leather boots. "How interesting. My name is Ivy Thornton. I own Storm Stables and this is my horse, Bolt."

The look on Ivy's face as she stared at Ember reminded Amara of a cat about to pounce on a mouse. "What do you want?" she said warily.

"Zara tells me Jill believes that this pony has tremendous power." Ivy leaned forward. "Why don't you bring him to my yard?" she said, her tone persuasive. "Come and be part of my team."

Amara frowned. "I couldn't even if I wanted to. He's not my pony. He belongs to

Jill and Moonlight Stables."

Ivy laughed. "You don't know much, do you, girl? Elemental horses do not belong to anyone. Their only bond is with their True Rider. He will follow you if you come to Storm Stables." Her tone became coaxing. "I can make it worth your while. New tack, new clothes – my riders have only the best . . ."

Amara shook her head. "I wouldn't move for things like that. Ember and I like it at Moonlight Stables."

Ivy's face hardened. "Join me, girl."

"No," Amara insisted.

Ivy drew herself up. "You foolish child. You know nothing about the powers you are playing with. You must join me!"

Ember gave a furious snort and stamped on the ground. A ball of flames shot from his hooves straight at Ivy. Bolt, Ivy's horse, reacted instantly. She shied to one side and as the fireball crashed into the nearby bracken and brambles she lunged furiously at Ember, her ears pinned back and her teeth bared.

Ember leapt back to avoid being bitten. The sudden movement unseated Amara and she felt herself slip to the side. She grabbed desperately at his mane. "Ember!" she gasped. But he ignored her, swinging round and setting off at a gallop.

For one terrifying moment, Amara hung half on and half off his back, seeing Ember's hooves flash by just inches from her face, and then she lost her grip and crashed into the ground skidding along the grass.

She lay there, grabbing breaths to replace

the air that had been knocked out of her by the fall. Suddenly, Ivy Thornton was there beside her, looking down mockingly from Bolt's back. "It looks like the Fire Horse chose wrongly when he chose you!" she said with a harsh laugh. "Some True Rider you're going to be. He may well have special powers, but it's clear you have none!"

Amara felt the ground vibrate as Ember

came racing back to see if she was OK. In an instant, Bolt was gone, galloping away down the hill.

Ember thrust his muzzle down, anxiously nuzzling Amara's face.

Amara struggled to her feet. The area where the fireball had hit was now alight with flames. They were flicking from the undergrowth into the trees, the wood crackling as it burnt, smoke filling the air. Panic sharpened her senses and numbed the pain of her bruises. She staggered back, away from the blaze.

"Do something, Ember!" she cried.

He stamped his hooves but, to Amara's dismay, nothing happened. A branch exploded in the flames, sending out a shower of sparks. Amara shrieked and ducked.

Hearing hoofbeats, Amara swung round and saw Alex and Imogen galloping across the field towards her.

"Help!" Amara cried, pointing at the flames. "Ember can't stop the fire!"

Tide reared up and, for a moment, Amara saw her in her magical form as she transformed from a grey pony into a beautiful ice-blue horse with blue eyes and a flowing mane and tail that looked like sea foam. Tide stamped her hooves down into the ground and a deluge of rain fell, dousing the flames.

The fire hissed and spluttered, fighting against the water, but then the flames faded to nothing, leaving just a thick smoke hanging in the air.

Tide stamped her hooves again and the

rain stopped. Transforming back into her usual self, Tide panted, clearly exhausted.

"What just happened?" Alex demanded.

"Why did Ember lose control of his magic?" Imogen asked.

Amara felt close to tears, shaken by her fall and by the dangerous fire. Ember hung his head. "It just happened so fast. Ivy was saying stuff about wanting Ember for her stables and she was mean about me. Ember got mad and stamped his hooves and then that happened." She waved her hand towards the charred, smoking bushes.

Imogen took a deep breath. "Don't worry. The important thing is that you're OK."

"Yeah, Rose can regrow the plants," said Alex. He rode towards the blackened vegetation and concentrated for a moment, sitting very still on her back. Rose snorted and Amara felt a rush of relief as she saw new green shoots pushing through the burnt stumps. Five minutes later, the damage had all been repaired.

Amara hugged Ember. She was sure from the way he was hanging his head that he felt terrible about the fire getting out of control.

"We need to tell Jill about this," said Imogen. She caught the look of alarm in Amara's eyes. "We don't need to tell her about the fire or about you and Alex falling off," she said. "But we should at least tell her what Ivy said about wanting Ember."

They were far more subdued heading back to the stables than they had been setting out. Amara caught Alex and Imogen exchanging worried looks. She was sure they were thinking about the fire. Ember's magic was so powerful – powerful and dangerous. She dreaded to think what would have happened if Tide hadn't been there.

CHAPTER SEVEN

That night Amara slept badly. Her shoulder hurt from falling off and whenever she rolled on to it in the night, she woke up. It was only bruised but it was still painful. When she got up at six o'clock, she felt like she'd hardly slept at all.

"Today, you're going to do some bareback riding," Jill said when they all gathered for the training session that afternoon. "Off with those saddles."

Everyone jumped off and started taking their ponies' saddles off.

"Bareback riding?" Amara echoed, still sitting on Ember.

"Yes. Off you get," said Jill briskly.

"You'll be fine," Imogen said. "You rode bareback the other day."

But when Amara was sitting on Ember without a saddle, all she could think about was how she had fallen off him the day before and how much her shoulder ached. As he walked around the school, her muscles tensed and she leaned forwards, holding tightly to his mane.

"What are you doing, Amara?" said Jill. "Sit back and relax."

Amara really wanted to, but the memories of the day before were too vivid and when

Ember broke into a trot and she bounced and slipped, she cried out in alarm. He stopped, but everyone had turned to look at her and her eyes burned with embarrassed tears.

Jill came over. "Whatever's the matter?"

Amara swallowed. "I . . . um . . . I don't know."

Jill considered her for a moment. "All right, go and put Ember's saddle back on. But you know you need to be able to ride without a saddle or bridle to take part in the Moonlight Ritual? It's only a week away."

"I know." Amara nodded miserably.

"I'm sorry," she whispered to Ember as she got off to put his saddle back on him. He nuzzled her and she could see from his eyes that he was saying it didn't matter, but she knew it did. If she was too scared to ride him without a saddle then how could she ever hope to be a proper True Rider? Maybe Ivy Thornton was right and Ember had made a mistake by choosing her.

Amara was quiet for the rest of the day. When the others left, she said goodbye and went down to the meadow. Ember trotted over. She climbed the gate and put her arms around his neck. "Oh, Ember," she whispered, shutting her eyes and resting her cheek against his mane. "I'm sorry about earlier. I felt so scared. I'm useless. Ivy was right, I'll never be a good True Rider."

You will!

Amara's eyes blinked open. She still wasn't used to hearing his thoughts when he was in

pony form. *I can hear you.*

Ember lifted his muzzle to her face. *It's because our bond is strengthening, and it will strengthen even more if you trust me enough to take part in the Moonlight Ritual. I promise if you start to fall off again, I'll stop.*

Amara stroked him. She knew he meant it, but what if he forgot?

Why don't we try again now? Ember suggested. *You just need to trust me.*

Amara hesitated. *Not now. I'm . . . I'm tired.* She saw the disappointment in his eyes. She remembered the way the fire had got out of his control. They needed to work on his magic. *We could practise your magic instead?*

This time, it was Ember who hesitated. *Not tonight. I'm . . . I'm tired too.*

Seeing him avoid her gaze, Amara suddenly realised he was as scared of doing magic as she was of riding him bareback. Should she try and persuade him to practise his magic? But he hadn't tried to make her ride him without a saddle, and she didn't want to upset him. *No,* she decided, she wouldn't insist. She reached out and touched his face. They gazed at each other, neither of them speaking their thoughts.

"Maybe tomorrow will be a better day for us," Amara said softly.

I hope so, said Ember, nuzzling her hands.

When Amara got up the next morning, her dad was in the kitchen in his work clothes – he had a property maintenance business which meant he did anything from looking after people's gardens to repairing fences. "Off to the stables again?" he said, draining his cup of coffee.

"Of course," said Amara, putting some bread in the toaster.

"Amara Thompson, I officially pronounce you pony-crazy!" said her dad, giving her a hug. "Right, I'd better take your mum her cup of tea. I've made your lunch. It's in the fridge, don't forget it."

"Thanks." Amara quickly buttered the toast and pulled on her wellies. She'd eat her breakfast on the way so she could get to the stables early. She wanted to see if she and Ember could manage to talk again before she started helping with the riding school ponies.

She was walking down the lane, deep in thought, when she became aware of the sound of hooves. Looking round, she saw Zara, Daniela and the girl with dark brown hair from Storm Stables trotting towards her on the same three gorgeous ponies she'd seen them on two days ago. *Elemental horses,* she suddenly realised. Not normal ponies. That's why they're all so beautiful.

She waited for the girls to trot past her but

they didn't. They surrounded her. Amara's heart started to beat faster as she looked up at them. "What do you want?"

"So this is Amara?" said the brown-haired girl, her grey eyes narrowing.

"Yes. Amara, this is Shannon," said Zara. "Our new friend from Storm Stables." She smirked at Shannon. "I told you Amara wore shabby clothes, didn't I?"

"You were right. Look at the state of her!" said Shannon meanly.

Amara tried to walk between Zara and Daniela's ponies but the girls moved their ponies closer together.

"Let me past!" said Amara, frowning.

"How's Ember?" Zara said. "Are you enjoying being his True Rider?"

Amara wondered why she was asking. "Yes.

Why?" she said warily.

Zara leaned down towards her. "Well, don't enjoy it too much," she hissed, her voice full of venom. "According to Ivy you might not have an elemental horse for long."

A chill ran through Amara. "Ivy can't do anything. Ember would never choose to go to her stables and if she stole him, Jill would call the police."

"There's more than one way to steal an elemental horse's power," said Shannon.

"What do you mean?" Amara demanded as the three girls on their ponies exchanged knowing smirks.

"Amara?" Amara swung round. Her dad was walking down the lane towards her, a lunchbox in his hand. "Here, you forgot your lunch at home." He looked between the girls, a frown creasing his forehead. "Is everything OK here, girls?"

Zara giggled sweetly, her expression changing in the blink of an eye. "Everything's fine. Daniela and I used to ride at Moonlight Stables. We saw Amara and just stopped to say hi."

Amara saw her dad's face relax. "Ah, I see. Well, here you are, Ams," he said, holding out the lunchbox.

Zara motioned with her head for them all to carry on down the lane. "Bye, Amara."

"It was really nice to meet you," said Shannon.

"Hopefully see you soon," said Daniela in a sing-song voice.

They trotted away.

"Right, I'd better get to work," Amara's dad

said giving her a quick hug.

Amara nodded. "Thanks, Dad."

As he walked away, she watched Zara and the others ride into the woods, her stomach tying itself in knots. What had they meant when they said there was more than one way to steal an elemental horse's power?

CHAPTER EIGHT

Over the next few days, Amara's senses were on red alert, but to her relief there were no more encounters with any riders from Storm Stables. Jill told Amara not to worry about what Zara and Shannon had said, but to focus on her riding. "If you can take part in the Moonlight Ritual, it will help strengthen Ember's magic. The stronger he is, the more he will be able to look after himself."

Amara practised lots and conquered her

nerves enough to be able to ride at a walk and trot bareback, but as soon as Ember broke into canter, the fear that she was going to fall off always flooded back and she would shout to him to stop.

On Friday, the day before the Moonlight Ritual, Jill asked her to wait behind at the end of the training session. "Amara, I'm really sorry, but I just can't let you take part in the Moonlight Ritual," she said with a sigh. "The others will be galloping and it wouldn't be safe for you to try and do that at the moment."

Amara's throat tightened. She had been expecting Jill would make that decision but it was still really hard to hear.

"You do understand, don't you?" Jill said, her voice unusually gentle.

Amara nodded, not daring to speak in case she started crying.

"You can still camp out and see everyone off, you just can't take part in the ride. I'm sure by the next one, you'll be able to join in. Your riding is improving every day."

Amara tried to comfort herself with those words as she rode away.

Imogen and Alex were waiting when she reached the stable block.

"What did she say?" asked Alex.

Amara sighed. "We can't take part in the ride but I can still stay overnight with you."

Imogen squeezed her arm.

"At least you can camp," Alex said.

"And next time you'll be riding with us," said Imogen. "We'll make sure of it!"

It should have been fun setting up the three-person tent that Alex's parents had lent them, but although Amara smiled and joked with the others as they arranged their inflatable mattresses and sleeping bags, her heart felt heavy. It would have been so much more fun if she and Ember had been going out on the moonlight ride too. *Ember's having to miss out and it's my fault,* she thought. I wish I was braver. But the memory of falling off still burnt sharply in her mind.

As the sun set and the sky darkened to black, the others got their ponies ready. Jill was going with them on Apollo. Amara stood with Ember as they rode to the gate that led on to the lane. "We'll be about an hour," said Jill. "We'll walk up through the woods and then gallop along the ridgeway."

"Have fun!" Amara said, forcing a smile.

Her friends waved and rode into the lane, the ponies' hooves loud in the quiet of the night.

Once they had gone, Amara wrapped her arms around Ember's neck and buried her face in his mane, fighting back the tears.

He nuzzled her. *I'm sorry.*

She gave a little start of surprise. After he had spoken to her in the field the other

night, she had hoped they would be able
to talk whenever they wanted, but it didn't
seem to work like that. She could only hear
him occasionally. They had to be completely
focused on each other. She was glad the
magic was working now because hearing
him made her feel better.

*You've got nothing to feel sorry for. It's my
fault we've had to stay behind, not yours.*

*It is my fault because you can't trust me
after I made you fall,* he said.

I do trust you. It's just . . . Just . . . Amara
trailed off and sighed. The bitter truth
was that he was right. She didn't trust him
completely, not after what had happened,
but she didn't want to hurt his feelings.

*Maybe by the next Moonlight Ritual you'll
be happy to canter and gallop without a*

saddle, he said hopefully.

She nodded. *And maybe you'll be happy to do your magic again.*

Ember hadn't conjured any fire since the day on the hill when he had shot a fireball at Ivy without meaning to and set light to the trees.

If you'd picked Zara as your rider, you'd have been able to go on the Moonlight Ritual, Amara said.

He looked into her eyes. *But I didn't want Zara. I wanted you.*

So you're still happy you chose me? she asked anxiously.

Very. As long as we've got each other, nothing else matters.

Amara's heart swelled with love. *We'll always have each other,* she promised him.

She kissed his forehead and then said goodnight and went back towards the yard. She felt a lot happier after talking to him.

I'll get everything ready for when the others return, she thought as she walked through the silent yard to Jill's garden. *I'll get the marshmallows out and . . .*

She stopped dead in her tracks. An icy wave of fear had just crashed over her. She didn't know why. It had come from nowhere. She stood still, her heart beating wildly. What was going on? Why did she suddenly feel so scared?

She swallowed, trying to calm herself down, but one thought beat in her head. *Ember.* She was sure something was wrong.

She hesitated for one more second and then turned and ran back to the meadow.

This is crazy. I've just left him. He was fine, she thought as she ran. But she couldn't ignore the feeling that he needed her.

As she ran down the track, she heard the sound of a voice and the snort of a horse in the still night. She stopped, every hair on her body prickling. Someone was in the meadow! She crept forwards, keeping to the shadows. Rather than going to the gate, she pulled apart the branches of the hedge and peered through. Ice flooded her veins.

Ivy Thornton was in the meadow on Bolt! Next to her, Ember was wearing a rope halter that glowed with a strange pale blue light. Amara watched in horror as Ivy turned Bolt and led Ember towards the gate that opened on to the lane. To Amara's astonishment, she saw Ember shake his head once, as if trying

to resist, but then fall into step beside Bolt. Ivy's cruel mouth curved into a smile.

What was she doing with Ember? Why was he going with her so willingly? Amara saw that his eyes were strangely dull and her gaze fell on the glowing halter. *I bet that halter's got some kind of magic power,* she thought, her mouth dry. *It's stopping him fighting. But why's she taking him? She can't just steal him. Jill will get him back. Unless...*

Shannon's words from a few days ago echoed through her mind: *There's more than one way to steal an elemental horse's power.* Did Ivy have some other plan in mind – something magic?

Ember tried to stop, pulling away, resisting with all his might.

Ivy jerked the leadrope attached to the

halter. "Move it!" she ordered, kicking Bolt on. "I've only got an hour before they're back!"

An hour? An hour to do what? Amara's mind raced.

Ember planted his feet and shook his head as if trying to get the halter off. Ivy threatened him with her crop. Ember's ears flattened. Amara could tell he was trying to fight, but whatever the magic was, it was too strong and he gave in and walked on through the gate.

Amara had to do something. She turned and raced back up the path. If she cut through Jill's garden she could cut them off, and then . . . then . . . well, she didn't know what she'd do, but she wouldn't let Ivy take Ember!

Her breath came in gasps and she could feel tears creeping into her eyes but she blinked them away. There was no time to cry. She had to save Ember!

Racing through the garden, she scrambled over the gate. Sprinting down the driveway, she leapt out just as Bolt was about to pass.

"Let Ember go!" she gasped.

"Get out of my way, girl!" hissed Ivy from Bolt's back.

"No!" Amara shouted as Ember fixed his eyes pleadingly on her.

Ivy lifted her riding crop. "I said get out of my way," she said, her voice charged with menace. "Or I'll make you get out of my way!"

CHAPTER NINE

Amara's heart thudded into her ribs but she stood her ground. "I'm not letting you take Ember!"

Ivy swept her crop down. Amara dodged and at the same moment, Bolt lunged forwards, her teeth missing Amara's arm by millimetres. Amara staggered backwards in shock. Bolt lunged again. Giving a furious squeal, Ember managed to fight the magic long enough to throw himself at Bolt, knocking the bay horse to one side.

Ivy yelled, distracted as Bolt tumbled and tried to regain her balance. Seeing her chance, Amara threw herself at Ember's head, her fingers closing on the glowing halter. The magic rope burnt her fingers but she didn't let go. She pulled it over his ears and threw it at Bolt. Ember was free!

With a delighted whinny, Ember reared up, transforming into his magical form, his mane and tail bursting into flames and his front legs striking out. Bolt charged at him, the halter now tangled in her thick mane. Ivy's face was etched with fury and she lifted her crop again.

Ember struck out with his hooves, making Bolt swerve.

We have to get out of here! Amara realised.

As Ember landed on all four feet, Amara threw herself on to his back. "Go, Ember! Gallop!" she yelled, wrapping her hands in his flaming mane and planting herself firmly on his back. He was taller and broader in his magical form but he was still her Ember. Despite her fear, excitement rushed through her at the thought of riding him in his magical form. "We need to find the others!"

Are you sure? he asked.

Yes! Go!

Ember raced down the lane. Amara was so preoccupied with Bolt and Ivy that she didn't have time to worry about falling off. She leaned forward, urging him to go faster as he entered the woods.

Bolt charged after them but Ember managed to keep just ahead, his hooves thundering along the sandy track that led through the woods.

Glancing round, Amara saw Ivy free the halter from where it was caught in Bolt's mane. With a whinny, Bolt instantly transformed, becoming a horse of smoke and darkness with lightning crackling around her hooves.

She shot past Ember and stopped in front of them, blocking the way. Ember halted so abruptly that Amara slipped to one side.

"Ember!" she gasped, terrified for a moment that he was about to swing round and set off again at a flat-out gallop. But he'd learned his lesson and he stood statue-still as she struggled to straighten herself.

"I will have that horse!' hissed Ivy. She pointed at Ember from Bolt's back. "I will drain his power and use it to make Bolt's lightning magic even stronger. You can have him back afterwards but I will have his magic."

Amara stared at her in horror. "You can't do that!"

Ivy's laugh cut through the air like a knife. "Oh, I can. If I can get him back to my stables while the full moon shines, I will be able to perform the Stealing Curse to take his power. Then he will have nothing left." She held up the eerie glowing halter, taking care it didn't touch Bolt. "As soon as this is back on him, he will not be able to fight me or use his magic and he will have to do as I say."

Amara looked round wildly.

"Don't even think about trying to escape," warned Ivy. "Bolt is faster and will outrun him in a second." Her pale eyes glittered with malice. "Give up, girl. Your horse's powers are going to become mine."

Bolt stepped closer, lightning crackling around her hooves.

Amara's heart pounded. *Ember, use your power!* she begged.

But the trees, the undergrowth, what if I lose control?

I'll help you. Trust me! Just do it, it's our only hope!

Ember stamped his front hooves. Amara felt a surge of magic rushing through her and every hair on her body seemed to spark as flames leapt up in a ring around Bolt and Ivy. With a furious whinny the dark bay horse reared up but the flames were already too high. They surrounded Bolt and Ivy like a

burning cage. Ivy screamed in frustration.

Amara felt Ember trembling as he struggled to contain the unnatural fire that was burning simply on thin air. *You're doing brilliantly, Ember. You're controlling it amazingly.* She kept talking to him and stroking him but all the time her mind was racing. Now what? Ember couldn't keep the fire burning for ever. *Maybe I could leave him here and run and try and find the others*, thought Amara. But no. She knew that wouldn't work because if she left Ember, he might lose control of his magic.

A spark flew up into the sky from the burning cage and an idea suddenly came to her.

Ember, do you remember when you first showed me your magic and you made flames shoot up into the sky?

Yes.

Can you do that? Just for a short time?

I ... I can try.

She felt him tense and then suddenly a column of flames blazed upwards from the top of the cage, reaching high up into the sky. Ember trembled and the flames died back down.

That's all I can do, Amara. I ... I'm almost out of magic.

She could feel his sides heaving as he drew in deep breaths. His legs were shaking and to her horror she saw that the flames around Bolt and Ivy were starting to fade.

Keep going, please keep going, she begged him.

Ember focused on Bolt and Ivy and the

fire grew brighter again but Amara knew he couldn't keep it burning for much longer. *Oh please,* she thought desperately. *Please let my plan work!*

"Amara!" Hearing a yell, she looked up the hill to the right. A wave of relief hit her as she saw the Moonlight Stables ponies and riders appearing through the trees! They had seen Ember's column of fire and realised something was going on! The four elemental horses were now all in their true forms – Tide with her ice-blue coat and mane and tail like sea foam; Rose with green eyes and a mossy green mane and tail that were covered in wildflowers; Sirocco with silver eyes and a wind that threw his mane and tail around; and Cloud, who had blue eyes and ribbons of water vapour swirling around her. Taking

in the scene below them, they came crashing
down the slope through the trees towards
Amara, with Jill and Apollo in the lead.

"Are you OK?" exclaimed Jill as they reached Ember.

"We saw a column of flame," said Jasmine.

"Ivy came for Ember. She wanted to take his power with some kind of curse!" Amara burst out.

Ember gave a shudder, his magic suddenly fading. Amara could feel the fire going out. But she knew he'd done enough – they'd done enough. They'd stopped Ivy from taking his power, and with Jill and the other riders now beside them, they were safe. Ember had controlled the fire so well that neither Ivy nor Bolt had even the smallest burn, but they both looked shaken and angry.

Jill's voice was cold as ice as she pointed at them. "Go!" she commanded. "Leave this place! And leave Ember and Amara alone if you know what's good for you."

Ivy hesitated but Amara could see the doubt in her pale blue eyes as she looked at the line of elemental horses. Bolt was strong and powerful, but she was completely outnumbered. "One day your horses' powers will all be mine!" she hissed, then she clapped her heels to Bolt's sides and the dark bay horse raced away.

Amara breathed out a trembling gasp. The other Moonlight Stables riders quickly surrounded her and Ember, all asking questions.

"What happened?"

"What was Ivy doing here?"

"Are you OK?"

Amara explained everything that had

happened with Ivy and Bolt.

"You were so brave standing up to Ivy like that," said Imogen as she heard how Amara had tried to stop Ivy taking Ember away.

Jill nodded. "And it took real courage to gallop Ember bareback when you were so scared of doing that."

"I wasn't the brave one," said Amara, leaning down and hugging Ember, whose breathing had just about returned to normal. "Ember was amazing. He didn't want to use his power, but it was the only thing that could stop Ivy so he did. And he controlled it brilliantly."

Because you were with me, Ember said to her. He nuzzled her hands. No one else could hear him. *I couldn't have done it without you. I love you, Amara.*

And I love you, she told him, smiling.

"What was the halter that Ivy was using?" Jasmine asked Jill. "How did it stop Ember using his magic?"

"It must have been made out of binding magic," Jill said. "When something made from binding magic touches an elemental horse, it stops them from using their powers. Only the person who makes a rope of binding magic can handle it without being burnt." She looked grim. "I don't think this is the end of it. Ivy's obsessed with power and will clearly do anything to get it."

"We'll stop her, whatever she tries next," said Amara determinedly, and Ember snorted in agreement.

"Definitely!" said Alex.

"No way is she getting any of our horses'

powers," said Imogen.

"Moonlight Stables all the way!" said Jasmine, high-fiving Ollie.

Jill smiled at them. "I agree! And now how about we get on with the Moonlight Ritual? I think strengthening the horses' magic is even more important after tonight." She gave Amara a sideways look. "You've galloped Ember bareback, so how do you feel about joining in? Do you want to?"

"Oh yes!" Amara said in delight.

They all headed back up the wooded hillside until they reached the ridgeway at the top where the trees gave way to grass. The moon was a round white disc in the cloudless, velvet-black sky and the bright stars clustered together in their constellations. The air was crisp and Amara

took a deep, long breath. Ember's back
was warm and now she had got used to his
movement she felt secure and relaxed. *If I
start to slip, he'll stop,* she thought. *I trust
him completely.*

And I trust you. He nuzzled her knee.

Happiness bubbled up inside Amara.

"Are you ready?" Jill asked them.

They all nodded eagerly.

"Then off you go!"

With whoops and cries, the five True
Riders all urged their ponies on along the
ridgeway. As Amara galloped beside her
friends, she felt the power surging from the
moonlight into Ember. His mane and tail
blazed suddenly, more brightly than ever as
his power was renewed, and her skin felt like
it was sparkling.

And this is just the beginning, she thought. *We've still got to learn how to use Ember's power for good. We've got so many more adventures to come!*

Surrounded by the pulsing current of magic, she and her beautiful elemental horse raced across the ridgeway while high above them the stars twinkled and the silver moon shone in the inky night sky.

The End

A message from Linda...

I really hope you've enjoyed reading about the adventures Amara and Ember have with the rest of the Moonlight Riders gang. I absolutely love writing about ponies and magic – they're two of my favourite things in the world!

It's also been great to write about mounted games. A few years ago I found myself managing our local Pony Club team when my daughter started competing on her gorgeous palomino pony, Angel. We really weren't very good compared to the other teams, but the boys and girls who were in the team trained really hard, became firm friends and had a huge amount of fun together. I can honestly say that some of my best pony memories were with that team, whether it was cheering the riders over the line or picnicking afterwards with Angel stealing everyone's sandwiches!

Anyone who competes in mounted games will realise that I've not been strictly accurate with my description of how mounted games competitions work. They're usually not run as local leagues, but I hope you will forgive me for making up a local league that the Moonlight Riders gang compete in. For anyone who has access to a pony and thinks they might like to try mounted games I would say 'GO FOR IT!'. You will have SO much fun!

Join the Moonlight Riders on
their next adventure in . . .
STORM STALLION
Read on for a sneak peek!

Amara ran down the path to the gate that
led to the meadow, the early morning dew
soaking into her trainers. There had been
a storm in the night, and branches lay
scattered across the grassy track, but the
wind had faded now and everything felt
fresh and bright.

Reaching the gate, Amara's gaze flew to
the eight beautiful ponies who were grazing
at the far end of the meadow – one grey, one
palomino, one bay-and-white, two chestnuts,
another bay, one grey-and-white and one
sleek black with a glossy mane.

"Ember!" she called.

The coal-black pony lifted his head. A

whinny burst from him and Amara felt fireworks of happiness exploding inside her as he cantered to meet her, his coat gleaming in the rays of the April sun. She didn't even stop to open the gate but scrambled over it to get to him.

Ember skidded to a halt and gently thrust his head against her chest. Amara wrapped her arms around his neck, resting her forehead against his and breathing in his sweet smell.

You're here very early, Amara. Ember's mouth didn't move but she could hear his thoughts as clearly as if he had spoken aloud.

The wind woke me up in the night. I couldn't get back to sleep so I thought I'd come and see you. She loved living just down the lane from the stables. It made visiting

Ember very easy! *Let's do some magic before everyone else gets here.*

Ember snorted in delight. Like all the horses in the meadow, he was an elemental horse – a horse with magical powers. His power was fire, while the others could do things like make plants grow, make it rain or conjure sandstorms. There were elemental horses all over the world. They chose boys or girls to be their True Riders, someone who could help them learn how to control their magic, then worked together to do good.

Let's do some magic now! Ember said.

A thrill ran through Amara as Ember cantered away, reared up and transformed from a beautiful pony into a majestic horse. His soft mane and tail changed into red and orange flames and his eyes glowed with golden fire. She loved seeing him in his magical elemental form! Running over to him, she grabbed his fiery mane and vaulted on to his back. The magic flames tickled her skin but didn't burn her. She dug her knees into his sides. "Gallop, Ember!" she cried.

Ember raced away around the meadow. Amara shouted out loud with excitement. Only a few weeks ago, she had been scared to ride Ember without a saddle but now she trusted him, and she loved the moments when she was able to gallop on him while he was in his true form. Her long brown plaits flew out behind her and she felt her body tingle with the magic that was flowing through him.

Skidding to a halt near a fallen branch which had split from an oak tree in the night,

Ember stamped his front hooves. A ball of fire flew at the bough and as it hit it, the wood burst into flames. The fire blazed up, reaching towards the blue sky. The ponies grazing at the other end of the meadow raised their heads to watch.

Hold on tight, Ember told her.

Amara grabbed his mane as he galloped forward and jumped high over the branch before turning and stamping his hooves again, controlling the flames and making them shrink smaller and smaller until they flickered and went out, leaving just a cloud of grey smoke floating in the air.

The other ponies whinnied with excitement. It was very difficult to control an element as strong as fire.

"That was brilliant, Ember!" Amara cried.

Ember changed back into his pony form.
He was panting slightly – doing magic
used a lot of energy – but Amara could feel
happiness coursing through him. *You're so
much better at controlling your magic now
than you used to be,* she told him.

He turned his head to nuzzle her leg.
That's because I've got you to help me.

She patted his neck. *I don't really do
anything.*

*You believe in me and trust me; that makes
all the difference.*

Leaning forward, Amara put her arms
round his neck and buried her face in his
silky mane. She was so lucky he'd chosen her
to be his True Rider!

She hugged him for a long moment and
then dismounted. *I'd better see if Jill needs*

any help clearing up after the storm, she told him.

Moonlight Stables, where Ember and the other elemental horses in the meadow lived, was owned by Jill Reed. Jill had been a True Rider when she was younger but her horse, Shula, a Fire Horse like Ember, had died in a dreadful accident. Jill had made it her life's work to try and help other elemental horses find their True Riders.

To be continued . . .

True Rider: Amara Thompson

Age:
10

Appearance:
Brown hair and blue eyes

Lives with:
Parents

Best friend:
Kalini

Favourite things to do:
Anything with horses, drawing and reading pony stories

Favourite mounted game:
Bending race

I most want to improve:
Vaulting on and off at speed and getting my handovers right

Elemental Horse: Ember

Colour:
Black

Height:
14.1hh

Personality:
Loving, lively, hot-tempered

Pony breed:
Welsh section B x Thoroughbred

Elemental appearance:
Golden eyes, swirling mane and a magical, fiery tail

Elemental abilities:
Fire Horse - Ember can create fires, make things burst into flame and cast fire balls from his hooves

True Rider: Imogen Fairfax

Age:
10

Appearance:
Light brown hair and hazel eyes

Lives with:
Mum, Dad, two brothers Will (17) and Tim (15), Minnie our cockapoo

Best friend:
Alex

Favourite things to do:
Anything with horses, walking Minnie, helping at my gran's teashop

Favourite mounted game:
Mug shuffle

I most want to improve:
My accuracy in races

Elemental Horse: Tide

Colour:
White-grey

Height:
14.1hh

Personality:
Thoughtful, sensitive and kind

Pony breed:
Arab x Welsh

Elemental appearance:
Blue eyes, silver-blue coat and a flowing sea foam mane and tail

Elemental abilities:
Water Horse - Tide can make it rain and manipulate bodies of water to create waves, whirlpools and waterspouts

True Rider: Alex Brahler

Age:
II

Appearance:
Black hair and dark brown eyes

Lives with:
Mum, Dad, sister Frankie
(15) and our chocolate Labradors,
Scooby and Murphy

Best friend:
Imogen

Favourite things to do:
Anything with horses, playing
football, cross-country running,
climbing and swimming

Favourite mounted game:
Five-flag race

I most want to improve:
Being more patient in
competitions so I'm not
eliminated by starting races
before the flag falls!

Elemental Horse: Rose

Colour:
Bright chestnut with flaxen
mane and tail, a white blaze
and four white socks

Height:
14.2 hh

Personality:
Patient, calm, confident

Pony Breed:
Welsh section C

Elemental appearance:
Bright green eyes, a mossy green
mane and tail covered in flowers

Elemental abilities:
Earth Horse - Rose can make plants
and flowers grow

Night Rider: Zara Watson

Age:
II

Appearance:
Blonde hair and green eyes

Lives with:
Mum most of the time
and Dad some of the time

Best friend:
Daniella (my cousin)

Favourite things to do:
Riding, playing tennis, shopping,
pamper sessions

Favourite mounted game:
Bottle race

I most want to improve:
Nothing, I'm good at everything

Elemental Horse: Scorch

Colour:
Bright chestnut with a white blaze

Height:
14.2hh

Personality:
Lively, mean, impatient

Pony Breed:
Show Pony x Thoroughbred

Elemental appearance:
Red eyes, mane and tail of dark
flickering flames

Elemental abilities:
Fire Horse - although not as
powerful as Ember, Scorch can heat
things up and cause small fires

Moonlight Riders

Meet all the True Riders of Moonlight
Stables and their amazing elemental horses!

Do you have what it takes to become a True Rider?